It's Up to You, Griffin!

by Susan T. Pickford

Illustrated by
Marcy Dunn Ramsey

TIDEWATER PUBLISHERS
Centreville, Maryland

One afternoon Mother Nature happened upon one of her
glorious autumn country scenes. She sat down on a lovely
hillside to delight in all her beautiful colors.

"It's got to be the prettiest sight I've ever seen," came
a voice at her feet.

Mother Nature looked down with a start. There sat a
fuzzy groundhog with kindly brown eyes.

"Why, Mr. Groundhog! You certainly surprised me,"
she said.

"So sorry, Mother Nature . . . I just couldn't help popping out again to admire your handiwork. Winter nap time is calling, but I had to take one last peek." The groundhog's eyes drooped a little, and he smiled.

Mother Nature was pleased. She knew the little ground-hog's appreciation of her gifts was real. "What's your name, little one?"

"Forgive me for not saying so before. I'm Griffin. My manners seem to be a little sleepy too!" He sounded a bit embarrassed.

"Dear Griffin . . . It so happens that I need a helper . . . someone who is dependable and wants to share his discoveries with others."

Griffin was so excited! Imagine, the grandest lady, Mother Nature, was talking to *him!* She was even suggesting that he help her in some small way. He leaned forward, hanging on every word.

"This tiny place . . . Winter-Begone, isn't it? It's nestled between these wooded hills, and the sun shines on it just so. I would like this to be the official spot for spring to begin. But I need someone who's quite responsible. He must make certain to wake up early to let the other animals know that winter is over. This is an important job I'm talking about."

She looked slyly at Griffin. "Do you think *you* could be in charge of this?"

Griffin just about fell all over himself trying to scurry
out of his hole. He knelt by the elderly lady.

"Oh, Mother Nature! It would be such an honor to serve
you! Of course, I'll do it!" he beamed.

That's how it became Griffin's job to wake up in
February to prepare the world for spring's arrival.

At Thanksgiving the groundhogs got together to enjoy all the foods they'd gathered and to give thanks for their winter homes. It was a festive night of celebration before their long winter's slumber. Griffin was the guest of honor, and the groundhogs presented him with an alarm clock with a gift tag attached.

FOR GRIFFIN

Griffin's pals drew away from the crowd after the feast.
"You must be thrilled to be chosen by Mother Nature
herself," exclaimed Nancy.

"Just thinking about it gives me goose bumps," giggled
Katie.

"You must be very brave," commented Hugo.

Griffin somehow heard Hugo through the chatter. Curiously he asked, "Why, Hugo, whatever makes you think I must be brave simply to wake up first?"

"Surely you must be afraid of all those hungry foxes and wolves. I'll bet after hunting for food for months they'd be right happy to see you poke your nose out. They might just gobble you up!"

Griffin shrugged this off. "I'm sure those beasts have better things to do than sit around and wait for me to wake up."

"I wouldn't be too sure. And what about weasels and bobcats? Gosh, Griffin . . . all those animals would frighten me to death!" Hugo said.

Griffin pretended not to be too interested. He didn't like having these new problems to consider, especially since he'd have to face them alone. "Oh, you're just letting your imagination run away with you, Hugo," he said, and then he decided to forget the conversation.

Later that night, Griffin was getting ready for bed. All
the disturbing things Hugo had said kept bothering him.
While he was carefully winding his new alarm clock, he
nervously looked around his usually cozy burrow. Griffin
felt as if he had so much depending on him. Spring and
summer were depending on him, and he had to face all
those scary foxes and wolves and such by himself.

The animals grew in his imagination. Their teeth got longer. Their claws grew. Their bodies started to change into terrifying monsters. Griffin huddled in his nest, afraid of his own thoughts.

"It's not really like that . . . they're just other animals," he whispered, trying to convince himself. "And there's no way they'll be sitting there waiting for me. I'll just be really careful when I come out."

With this, Griffin began to feel a little better. He was also very tired and soon he fell fast asleep.

Wintertime came. The land turned white with snow.
Christmas came and went and then the start of the new
year. Many animals hibernated in their burrows enjoying
the winter's rest.

Griffin, though, tossed and turned. His dreams were
not at all pleasant, and his sleep was anything but restful.
His responsibility and fears invaded his thoughts. Visions
of huge monsters waiting at the entrance to his home made
him shiver in his sleep.

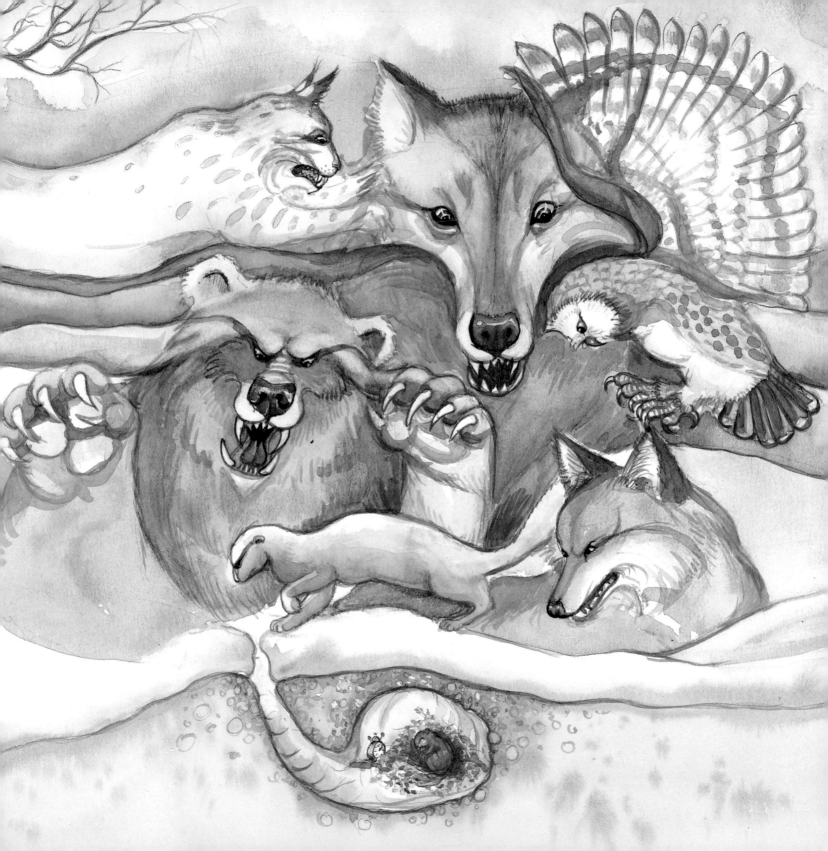

BRRRRRRRRRIIIIIIIINNNNNNNNGGGGGGGG!

Griffin sprang from his nest and hit the alarm clock button. He was still groggy with sleep and he wasn't even sure where he was. Then suddenly it came to him.

"Oh, my gosh, spring is waiting for me!"

Griffin dashed up to the opening of his burrow. What kind of a day would the first day of spring be? He pushed away the sticks and leaves that had fallen across his doorway.

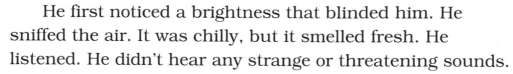

He first noticed a brightness that blinded him. He sniffed the air. It was chilly, but it smelled fresh. He listened. He didn't hear any strange or threatening sounds.

"OK, Griffin," he said to himself. "It's time. You've just got to make yourself do it."

With that, Griffin sprang out of the hole.

It was a cold but beautiful day. The sun gleamed off the drifts of snow. The light was overwhelming, and Griffin squinted. It didn't help much. After being in the dark for months, his eyes didn't adjust quickly.

He looked down, rubbing his eyes. When he started to open them, his surroundings were still blurry. But he *could* see the huge shadow that was right in front of him— a monster with spiky fur and outstretched arms!

Griffin's heart nearly stopped. He turned and bolted back into his tunnel before he even drew another breath.

"Oh, my gosh! Oh, my gosh!" was all he could say in his panic. Griffin didn't stop until he was back in his nest with leaves piled over his head.

"What am I going to do?" His breathing was beginning to slow. "What in the world am I going to do?"

How was he going to wake the little forest creatures for
spring if there were monsters waiting for him to come out?
Mother Nature was going to be so disappointed! Griffin's
eyes filled with tears.

"I won't do it! I just won't do it! If I so much as go near
the doorway, that monster will get me for sure!"

Griffin jumped up and paced back and forth, chewing
his nails. Never once did it cross his mind that the sun on
his back in the early morning had made the huge shadow
from his own body.

"I'm not going to do it! If I tried and got eaten up, I
couldn't wake anyone up anyway." He crawled back into
his nest and lay there worrying about not doing his duty.

As Griffin dozed off, he was feeling bad about how the world was counting on him and how he was letting it down. All of the animals would sleep and sleep, and they would miss spring and summer because of him.

Suddenly his eyes flew open. It shocked him to look at the clock and see that several weeks had gone by.

"Oh, how can this be?" he moaned. "Mother Nature believed in me . . . I must be strong. I can do this!"

Griffin once again ran to the entrance of his home. He leaped out of the hole without another thought. The air was crisp and cool. The grass was thick and green. The breeze brushed against his fur. The day was slightly cloudy and the sun was momentarily hiding. No monster appeared before him. Griffin was so happy he flung his arms around himself, giving himself a gigantic hug.

"I did it!" he shouted. "I DID IT! Wake up, world. It's a beautiful spring day!"

The sun even smiled as it came out from behind a little cloud.

"WAKE UP!" Griffin called, and he danced across the field. "Hey, everybody, WAKE UP!"

Every bat, bear, and beetle, every frog, snake, and turtle; they all opened their sleepy eyes and raised their rested heads. Indeed, it was spring.